10

Weekly Reader Presents

Best Friends

By Jocelyn Stevenson · Pictures by Sue Venning

Muppet Press

Holt, Rinehart and Winston

NEW YORK

Copyright © 1984 by Henson Associates, Inc.
Fraggle Rock, Fraggles, Muppets, and character names are trademarks of Henson Associates, Inc.
All rights reserved, including the right to reproduce this
book or portions thereof in any form.
Published by Holt, Rinehart and Winston,
383 Madison Avenue, New York, New York 10017.

Library of Congress Cataloging in Publication Data

Stevenson, Jocelyn.
Best friends.
Summary: Mokey, a quiet Fraggle, and her best friend
Red, a noisy Fraggle, have very different experiences
along the way to Brushplant Cave.
[1. Puppets—Fiction.   2. Friendship—Fiction]
I. Venning, Sue, ill.   II. Title.
PZ7.S8476Be 1984   [E]   84-6859
ISBN: 0-03-000723-2
First Edition
Printed in the United States of America
1 3 5 7 9 10 8 6 4 2

ISBN 0-03-000723-2

This book is a presentation of
Weekly Reader Books.

Weekly Reader Books offers book clubs for children
from preschool through junior high school.

For further information write to:
Weekly Reader Books
4343 Equity Drive
Columbus, Ohio 43228

Weekly Reader Books offers several exciting
card and activity programs. For information,
write to WEEKLY READER BOOKS, P.O. Box 16636,
Columbus, Ohio 43216.

Best Friends

MOKEY Fraggle and Red Fraggle are best friends.

Mokey is a quiet Fraggle. She likes to think.
She likes to dream. She likes to watch what's going
on around her.

Red is a noisy Fraggle. She likes to swim. She likes to run. She likes to yell "WHOOPEE!" very loud.

Mokey and Red are not alike, but they like each other a lot.

One day, in the middle of painting an important picture of Red, Mokey's paintbrush fell apart.

That meant only one thing: Mokey had to make a trip to Brushplant Cave, deep inside Fraggle Rock.

"You can't go there alone!" Red said when Mokey told her.

"I can't?" asked Mokey.

"No," Red answered. "It is too dangerous. I'll go

with you and protect you. After all, what are best friends for?"

"That's wonderful!" Mokey cried. "We'll have so much fun!"

Red didn't think they would have fun at all. She knew that to get to Brushplant Cave, they would have to pass the den of the terrible Gagtoothed Groan.

But Red was a brave and daring Fraggle. "If we're going, let's get going!" Red said bravely, and off they went down a dark and winding tunnel.

The first place Mokey and Red passed was the
Cavern of the Creeping Crocus.
"Don't these flowers smell wonderful!" Mokey sighed.
Red didn't think the flowers smelled wonderful at all.

She was too busy untangling herself from their clinging vines.

"Don't worry, Mokey," Red gagged bravely, "I'll protect you!"

"Oooh, look! Isn't that spiderfly beautiful?" Mokey cried, leaping over the Great Gorge.

Red didn't think the spiderfly was beautiful at all.

She was too busy thinking how deep the Great Gorge was.
"Don't worry, Mokey," Red gasped bravely, "I'll
protect you!"

"I don't know why no one likes to come here," Mokey said as they tiptoed through the Falling Rock Zone. "It's such an interesting place!"

Red didn't think it was interesting at all. She was too busy digging herself out of a pile of rocks.

"Don't worry, Mokey," Red grunted bravely, "I'll protect you!"

Red and Mokey were getting very close to the den of the horrible, terrible, awful, bad, disgusting Gagtoothed Groan. "Isn't this exciting?" Mokey whispered.

Red didn't think it was exciting at all. She thought it was scary. (Even brave Fraggles like Red get scared sometimes.)

"Don't worry, Mokey," Red said bravely, "I'll protect you!"

"It's hard to believe a horrible, terrible, awful, bad, disgusting monster lives in a place as beautiful as this. Isn't it, Red?" Mokey skipped past the dark den of the Gagtoothed Groan.

"*Groan!*" groaned the Groan.

Red didn't think it was hard to believe at all. "Don't worry, Mokey," Red gulped bravely, "I'll protect you!"
Suddenly the Groan leaped out and grabbed Red by the pigtails.

"Don't worry, Mokey," Red cried bravely, "I'll protect you!"

"You horrible Groan!" Mokey cried. "Let go of my best friend!" And Mokey bopped the Groan on the nose.

The Groan was so surprised that it let Red go.

"Go away, you...you...Gagtoothed Groan!" Red cried. And the Gagtoothed Groan went away, groaning.

"Poor little Groan," said Mokey.

Red didn't think it was poor at all.

"Good thing I was here to protect you, Mokey," Red said bravely.

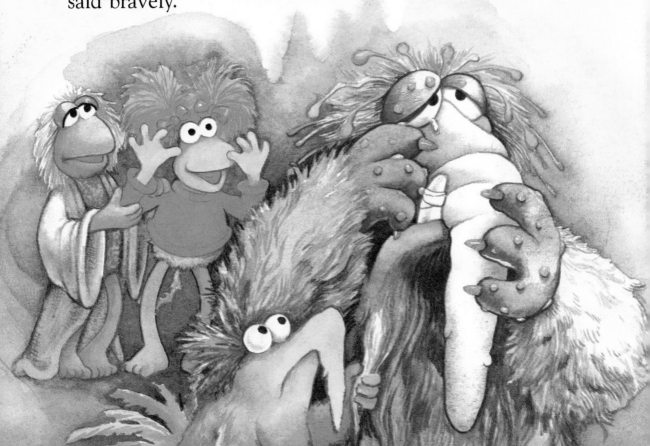

Red and Mokey finally reached Brushplant Cave.
"What an inspiring journey!" sighed Mokey.
Red didn't think it had been an inspiring journey at all.
"I'm glad I was there to protect you," Red said bravely.

Mokey spent the rest of the day finding the right brushplant to use for her paintbrush.

Red spent the rest of the day recovering from bravely protecting her friend.

"Oh, Red, thank you so much for protecting me," said Mokey.

"Zzzzzzzzzzzzz," Red snored bravely.